THE POWERFUL FOUR

SPRING BREAK ISLAND

I0623607

written by
Sophie Cole

illustrated by Glori Alexander

Chapter 1

The Story Begins

It was a perfectly normal day in Miami until it wasn't. I should know. I was there. Hey, I'm Mary Ann Sherman. I'm going to tell you this story about my friends: Kate Tanner, Bella Walker, Lynn Wood, and me. This story is something that changed our lives forever. Before I start, let me tell you about my friends and me. Kate is thirteen years old, and she has brown eyes, fiery red hair, freckles galore, and she's a total tomboy. Bella is fourteen years old and has green eyes and chocolate brown hair with her tips dyed blue; she's also a tomboy like Kate. Lynn is fourteen years old, and she has blue eyes, chestnut brown hair, and always has the most impressive and fashionable wardrobe. I am thirteen years old, and I have blue eyes and honey blonde hair with pink streaks running through my hair. If you don't mind me saying so, I suggest you sit back and relax because this is a long story…

It all started the day before spring break. My friends and I were walking to school when Lynn said, "Tomorrow is spring break. What do you guys want to do?"

"I'm not sure," answered Kate, Bella, and me.

"Camping?" suggested Bella.

"Not a big fan of camping," Lynn replied.

"Rock climbing?" asked Kate.

"I'm scared of heights," I replied.

"Mani-pedi?" asked Lynn.

"Not in a million billion years," said Kate firmly.

I giggled and wrapped my arm around Kate's shoulder. It's no secret that out of the four of us, Kate and I are closer to each other, and Bella and Lynn are closer to each other. Finally, we rounded the corner, and our school building came into view.

"Can we talk about this later? I promised Mrs. Tidwell I'd help her with something before homeroom," I said as I started walking away.

I walked through the crowded hallway of the school and then turned left into my homeroom. There I saw my teacher Mrs. Tidwell, a very kind-hearted woman in her early fifties. As I closed the door, I said, "Hi, Mrs. Tidwell, what was it you wanted my help with again?"

Mrs. Tidwell had a warming smile and said softly, "Hello, Mary Ann. Could you help me with my computer?"

I'm not an expert in computers, but I know enough about them to help out anybody who needs it.

"Okay, how can I help?" I asked.

"Well, I'm going to show a video in my class after homeroom, and I don't have enough time between classes to set it all up, so I was wondering if you could help me hook up my computer to the screen," answered Mrs. Tidwell.

Hooking up the computer, setting up the video, and watching it once to ensure it was working correctly took about ten minutes. Thank goodness it didn't take any longer because as soon as I was done, the bell rang to announce that homeroom was starting. I took my usual seat in the third row between Nicole Walters and Oliver King, got papers and a pencil, and studied for my math test. I hate math, so homeroom dragged on very slowly. Finally, the bell rang to announce that homeroom was over, and it was time for science. I quickly put away my papers and pencil, got my science books out of my locker, and went to Science class. This part of the story isn't important, so I'll just skip this part. Six tedious hours later, the school day was over. I put away books in my locker and walked to the school doors.

"Hey," I said once I met my friends at the door.

"Hey, ready to go home?" asked Kate.

"Yes," Lynn, Bella, and I replied. So, my friends and I started walking home, and once we got to our neighborhoods, we went our different ways.

"I'm home!" I called once I walked through the front door to my house.

"Hey Mary," replied both of my brothers, Brian and Mark. I turned around to see Brian and Mark with their eyes glued to the TV playing a video game. I giggled softly and went into the kitchen for a snack. I grabbed a granola bar and went upstairs to my room. Meanwhile, over at Lynn's house, something happened that decided what we would do for spring break…

Chapter 2

To Aunt Isabel's House, We Go

Lynn was sitting on her bed drawing in her sketchbook when her mom came in and said, "Lynn, I've got Aunt Isabel on the phone, and she wants to talk to you." So, Lynn set down her sketchbook, took the phone from her mom, and talked to her aunt.

"Hey," said Lynn.

"Hey, Pumpkin!" replied Lynn's aunt from the other end of the phone.

"How are you?" asked Lynn.

"Oh, I'm doing just fine; how would you like to come to stay with me for the week? It's a little lonely here when your uncle is out of town for work, and I haven't seen you in a while, so what do you say?" asked Aunt Isabel.

"Wow, really?!" exclaimed Lynn. "Can my friends come with me? We were trying to find something to do for spring break."

"The more, the merrier," replied Aunt Isabel.

Lynn's aunt lives on a small island in the Florida Keys, so Lynn and her older sister Hayley don't see their aunt and uncle very often. A few minutes later, Lynn said goodbye to her aunt and texted Kate, Bella and me to tell us the fantastic news.

"Guys! You'll never believe what just happened!" Lynn texted. She told us about the phone call and the trip we were going to go on. (If we get permission from our parents of course.)

"AWESOME!" I texted.

"GREAT!" texted Bella.

"THIS IS GOING TO BE AWESOME!" texted Kate. Thankfully we all got permission from our parents. Yay! We all started packing for our trip.

The next day my parents drove me to Lynn's house. Lynn's mom drove Kate, Bella, Lynn, and me to the docks, where we got on a boat called a ferry for an hour-long cruise to get to the Florida Keys to stay with Lynn's aunt. During the hour-long Cruise, my friends played Truth or Dare. Since I hated the game, I sat back, watched, and enjoyed the passing scenery. The hour went by quicker than you might think. Once the ferry was docked, my friends and I got our suitcases, hopped off the boat, and were greeted by Lynn's aunt.

"Aunt Isabel!" Lynn exclaimed, dropping her bags, and running over to hug her aunt.

"Lynnie Bear!" Aunt Isabel exclaimed while grabbing Lynn and giving her a bear hug. Lynn let go and introduced us to her aunt.

"Aunt Isabel, these are my friends, Bella Walker, Kate Tanner, and Mary Ann Sherman," said Lynn.

"Nice to meet you," I said.

"Hey," said Kate.

"Hi," said Bella.

"Hello girls, it's very nice to meet you," replied Aunt Isabel.

We talked for a few minutes, Lynn said goodbye to her mom, and we hopped into Aunt Isabel's car, and within fifteen minutes, we were in the driveway of a big old-fashioned house. On the front porch were two rocking chairs, a wooden round table, and beautiful flowers in flowerpots.

"You have a beautiful home, Miss Isabel," I commented.

Aunt Isabel chuckled softly and said, "Please call me Isabel. All my friends do, and a friend of Lynn's is a friend of mine." I smiled happily, and we all went inside. After we stepped into a beautiful white kitchen, Lynn's aunt said, "Make yourselves at home, girls,"

"Would you mind showing us our rooms, so we know where to put our stuff?" asked Bella.

"Certainly," Isabel replied.

Isabel showed Lynn and me to a small and cozy bedroom upstairs. The room had lavender purple walls, a window seat with beautiful white pillows, a small white dresser, and a bunk bed with lovely quilts the same color as the walls. Next, Isabel showed Kate and Bella to another small and cozy room downstairs with grey walls, two twin-sized beds with a small side table in between, a small dresser, and a small bookcase in the corner. Unpacking and getting settled in took about thirty minutes.

Lynn and I were sitting on the window seat in our room talking when Isabel called, "Lunch is ready!" We had a delicious peanut butter and jelly sandwich for lunch and then went to the beach. We all quickly changed into what we would wear to the beach. I wore a two-piece swimsuit with colorful flowers all over it and a sundress over it that was white with yellow sunflowers, Lynn wore a crop-top style bikini that was blue, and Bella wore a one-piece swimsuit with a cute giraffe on it. Kate, who thinks swimsuits are uncomfortable, just wore shorts and a red tank-top. Isabel stayed behind to clean the dishes while my friends and I went to the beach.

"Does anybody feel like going for a walk?" I asked.

"Sure," said Lynn.

"Okay, I'll go," said Bella.

"I guess I'll go too. I'm not dressed for swimming anyway," said Kate.

So, my friends and I walked around the beach, to the base of a mountain, when suddenly, "OH MY GOSH!" I cried.

Chapter 3

Lost In Light

"Mary, what's wrong?!" asked Kate, concerned. My friends crowded around me, and I pointed high up the mountain to a cave. A cave with a weird blueish green light shining from it!

"What is that?" asked Lynn.

"I don't know, but I'm about to find out," said Kate running to the side of the mountain where she started climbing it.

"KATE! STOP!" I screamed, trying to catch up with her. But unfortunately, she was so fast, there was no way I could. She reached the cave first and waited for the rest of us. Bella and Lynn were not far behind me, and pretty soon all four of us were standing there staring into the cave.

"Well...we're here," said Bella breathlessly. Then, acting before thinking, I slowly started walking into the cave. Kate, Bella, and Lynn followed. We walked in silence, all thinking our own thoughts. The farther we went, the darker it got. We were walking for about fifteen minutes when...THUD!

"Mary Ann, why did you walk into the wall?" Kate asked, trying not to laugh.

"Ha, ha, very funny," I said sarcastically. "It looks like this is as far as it goes," I said.

"We better go back anyway. Aunt Isabel will probably be looking for us by now," said Lynn.

So we started walking back. Since it was pitch-black in the cave, we got lost, and somehow we ended up separated from one another. All of us went different ways as we were trying to get out of the cave.

"Where do you think we are?" asked Lynn, still not realizing that she was alone. The same thing happened with Bella, Kate, and me. We started panicking when none of us could hear one another's reply. We started running and eventually ran into each other.

"OW!" we screeched. When we saw each other, I sighed with relief.

"Are you guys okay?" asked Lynn.

"Yeah," Kate, Bella, and I replied.

Then we realized there was a strange light that was not coming from the entrance of the cave and not from a hole in the cave. In fact, the light wasn't normal light at all. Instead, the light was a pinkish purple color, and it was coming from the floor.

"THE FLOOR!" I shrieked.

My friends looked down. We were standing on a pool of pinkish-purple water with a layer of glass on it! We screamed, the glass broke, and we fell in.

Chapter 4

Is This Actually Happening?!

Seconds later, we came up gasping for air.

"That's it, I am out of here," I said as I swam out of the pool and walked away. My friends quickly followed, and we left the cave within ten minutes. We quickly walked back to the beach, where we saw Isabel.

"There you girls are!" she cried, "I've been looking all over for you girls; you're soaking wet; what happened?"

"We just…went for a little swim that's all," said Bella.

"Even you, Kate? You're not even wearing a swimsuit," asked Lynn's aunt.

Kate was silent for a moment, then replied, "Um, yeah. I was walking along the shore while the girls were swimming, and I tripped over a rock and fell in the water."

"Okay…well, we better head back to the house and get you girls dried off," replied Isabel. So we walked home, cleaned up silently, and remained silent through dinner time. After dinner, my friends and I sat in the living room while Isabel was doing the laundry in the other room.

"Finally! Do you guys want to talk about what happened earlier in the cave?" I asked.

"I don't even know what happened," replied Bella.

"Well…we saw the light coming from a cave, we went into the cave, got lost, got separated, eventually found each other, found out we were standing on top of a pool with glass on top and fell in," Kate said thinking out loud.

"Is that normal?" asked Lynn slowly.

"I don't think so," I replied. Then, after a minute or two, Bella said, "Well, it's getting late, so I think I'll head to bed."

"Yeah, I'm going to go too. Goodnight Mary; Goodnight Lynn," said Kate, following Bella into the other room.

Not long after, Lynn and I decided to go to bed too. I went upstairs while Lynn went to tell her aunt that we all had gone to bed. After Lynn and I changed into our pajamas, I climbed into the bottom bunk. Lynn climbed into the top bunk, and so many thoughts were swirling around inside my head. I laid in bed an hour before finally getting to sleep, which was probably the same thing with the other girls.

The next morning, we all woke up to the fantastic smell of pancakes. We quickly changed out of our pajamas and raced to the kitchen.

"Good morning, girls," said Isabel once we entered the kitchen.

"Morning," the rest of us replied. As we sat at the table eating, we were all quiet, especially Bella.

"Are you okay, Bella?" I asked after a minute.

Bella looked up from her plate and said, "Huh? Oh yeah, I'm fine. I just have a headache. I think I'm going to go to my room for a bit."

Bella stood up, put her plate in the sink, and left the room. We finished breakfast as quickly as we could. The girls thought it would be relaxing for us to watch a movie together. So, they started setting everything up so we could watch our favorite movie. I went to check on Bella. When I peeped my head in through the door, I didn't see her.

I thought she was probably napping, so I quietly walked into the room, closed the door behind me, and walked over to her bed, but she wasn't there either.

I looked up and saw something, but I didn't know what it was, so I turned on the lights and saw that the thing that was floating in the air was, "BELLA!" I cried. Bella was floating above her bed, sound asleep!

Kate and Lynn came racing in after hearing me scream. When they saw Bella, they both screamed.

Our screams woke Bella up because she rubbed her eyes, sat up, and said, "What's going on? Why am I so high up?" Then she looked down and said, "Oh, I'm floating above my bed."

It must have taken a moment to sink in because a minute later, Bella cried, "I'M FLOATING ABOVE MY BED." Bella suddenly fell hard on the floor; I ran over and asked, "are you okay?"

"Yeah, I think so," Bella replied.

"So, um, that was weird...what now?" I answered.

None of us knew what to do, and it wasn't like we could have gone to Lynn's aunt about this. Finally, Kate calmly replied, "How about we think about this later, and for now, just watch the movie?" So that's exactly what we did. We sat on the couch in the living room and watched the movie. But none of us could concentrate on the movie. We were all thinking about Bella floating in the air.

After lunch, Bella was in her bedroom, Kate was sitting on the couch in the living room, Lynn was sitting in our bedroom, and I was sitting in the kitchen, all thinking our own thoughts when Bella texted us.

"Ummm...you guys might want to come to see this," Bella's text said.

Kate, Lynn, and I walked into Bella and Kate's bedroom and were all confused about why Bella wanted to see us. But when we walked into Kate and Bella's room, we found out why...

When we walked in, we saw Bella pacing nervously around her bed.

"Bella, what's wrong?" I asked. Bella stopped pacing and said, "I think you guys might want to sit down when I tell you what I'm about to tell you." Kate walked over and sat in a chair in the corner, and Lynn and I sat in front of her.

Bella faced a cup on the nightstand, held her arm out toward it, and the cup started floating! Then Bella raised her other arm, and a notebook lying next to the cup started floating too! A few seconds later, Bella placed the cup and the notebook back on the nightstand. We were all speechless.

"H-how did you do that?" I asked.

"I don't know," Bella replied, "I just hold my hands out and picture it in my mind, and it just happens."

We were all so amazed that we watched Bella play with her new powers for a long time.

The next day, my friends and I were sitting in the living room playing a board game when I noticed that Kate seemed upset. Kate had her head in her hands. So, I walked over, sat down next to Kate, and asked, "Kate, are you okay?"

Kate sat up and replied, "Not really. Am I the only one that feels extremely hot?"

I put my hand on Kate's forehead. "Oh, Kate, you have a fever. Do you feel okay?" I asked.

"Oh no, here comes Mary Ann, aka the helicopter parent," said Bella sarcastically.

"I'm not a helicopter parent. I just want to make sure my friends are okay," I replied.

"Anyway, Lynn, do you know where your aunt is?" Kate asked, getting back to the subject.

"I don't know, in the kitchen probably," Lynn replied. Without another word, I walked into the kitchen, only to find a note on the table left by Isabel. I picked up the note, walked back into the living room, and handed it to Lynn.

"Dear girls, I assume you've noticed I'm not home if you're reading this. Sorry I didn't tell you, but I had an appointment early in the morning, and I guessed you girls wouldn't want to come. Afterward, I'm going to run some errands. So I'll be home around 1:00 pm. XOXO Aunt Isabel," Lynn read aloud.

"Well, now what?" Bella asked.

"Lynn, do you know where your aunt's medicine cabinet is?" I asked.

"Above the sink in the kitchen," Lynn replied.

I walked into the kitchen, and a few seconds later, I walked back into the living room with a thermometer and a cold, wet cloth in my hands. I put the thermometer under Kate's tongue, and when I took the thermometer out of Kate's mouth, I saw that it read 101! I held the wet cloth against Kate's forehead.

"Does this help?" I asked.

"Well, I don't know, Mary Ann. The wet cloth has only been pressed against my forehead for five seconds!" Kate snapped.

"Sarcasm doesn't help the fever, Kathrine!" I snapped back. Kate sighed and flopped back as far as she could in the chair. (Which wasn't very far.) Just then, Kate's stomach grumbled loudly, and I said, "Let's go into the kitchen and get you something to eat." Without hesitation, Kate followed me into the kitchen.

"Okay, Kate, sit and relax, and I'll make you a grilled cheese," I said, gently pushing Kate into a chair. Kate didn't argue; she just did as she was told. I walked over to the gas stove and turned a little knob that said "ON" on one side and "OFF" on the other side. I turned the knob, but nothing happened.

"What the heck?" I said half to myself.

"What?" asked Kate.

"I'm turning the knob to the ON side, but nothing's happening," I replied. Then, Kate got up, walked over to me, placed her hand on the stove, and suddenly, the gas stove started! Kate and I both jumped back in shock as we watched the small flames.

"D-did I do that?" asked Kate.

"I think so," I replied.

Then Lynn and Bella walked in, and Lynn said sarcastically, "What, are you amazed by how a gas stove works?"

"No!" Kate snapped back. I explained to the girls what had happened.

"What?" Bella asked, confused.

Kate slowly walked toward the stove and held out her hand. I was about to ask what she was doing when suddenly, the small flames on the stove burst into one huge flame that covered most of the stove! I quickly pulled an oversized cup from the cabinet, filled it with water from the sink, and splashed it all over the flame. The fire went out instantly. My friends and I all breathed a sigh of relief.

"Nobody tells Isabel about this," Kate said.

"Agreed," Bella, Lynn, and I replied.

"Tell me what?" asked a voice from behind us. We all spun around to see Isabel standing in the kitchen, the front door still open. There were a few seconds of silence, but then I blurted out, "CUPCAKES!"

"Huh?" everybody else asked.

"We're making cupcakes for you. They were going to be a surprise for you, and we had planned for them to be decorated by the time you got home, but you're just so early that the cupcakes are still in the oven," I answered, making it up as I went.

"R-right! Um, Aunt Isabel, why don't you go and relax, maybe watch some TV? I'm sure the cupcakes will be done soon," said Lynn pushing her aunt out of the room."

The second Isabel was out of ear-shot, Kate grabbed my arm and angrily whispered, "Way to go, Mary Ann, now we have to make cupcakes!"

"Don't worry," I replied calmly. "I make cupcakes all the time. I can make cupcakes like that!" I snapped my fingers as I said the word, "that."

"Do you need any help?" Bella asked.

"Not with the cooking, but it would be helpful for the two of you to go help Lynn distract Isabel," I replied.

"Got it," Bella replied, grabbing Kate's arm and walking out of the room. I quickly grabbed all the things I would need to make the cake: a large bowl, mixer, flour, eggs, sugar, baking soda, and many other things. After that, the rest of the day was slow and quiet.

The next morning, I woke up refreshed, but outside was dark and gloomy, and so was Lynn.

"It's too bad it's so gloomy outside; we could have gone to the beach," I said, sitting on the window seat and staring out the window.

"That would only make today worse," Lynn said grumpily.

"What's wrong with you?" I asked.

"I'm in a bad mood," Lynn replied.

"Well then, I guess it's time for a visit from the Tickle Monster!" With that, I got up and pretty much pounced on Lynn and started tickling her. Lynn began laughing so hard that she was practically crying! I let go of Lynn and saw that outside had gone from dark and gloomy to sunny and beautiful.

"Huh?" I said aloud.

"What?" Lynn asked me.

"A minute ago, outside was dark and sad looking, and now outside, it's beautiful and sunny," I answered. Lynn and I raced to the kitchen, where we found Kate and Bella still in their pajamas. Lynn and I ran outside, Kate and Bella following with confusion.

"What are you guys doing?" Bella asked.

Lynn explained to them what had happened. Continuing to talk while walking, Lynn tripped over a rock and yelled angrily, "Stupid rock, I got my pj's all sandy!" Then the sky got all dark and gloomy again. Bella helped Lynn up, and Lynn dusted herself off.

"Come on, guys, let's go inside before it rains. Coming Mary Ann?" Kate asked.

"Huh? Oh yeah," I replied. When we got inside, we were greeted by Isabel.

"Oh, hello, girls. What were you doing out there?" Isabel asked.

"Oh, just getting some fresh air," Kate replied.

"Okay, well, go ahead and wash up. Breakfast is almost ready," Isabel instructed.

So, my friends and I did as we were told. We washed our hands in the bathroom, then went back into the kitchen, where five plates of French toast were already set down. Lynn sat down, took a sip of her apple juice, and sighed happily. Then I noticed that outside, the sky was no longer dark and gloomy but sunny and beautiful again.

"That's weird," I said as I walked toward the window.

"What?" asked Bella.

"Look," I answered. "First it was dark and gloomy, then it was sunny, then it was gloomy again, and now it's sunny again."

"How strange. I think I will watch the news and see what the weather will be like for the rest of the day," said Isabel. Isabel got up and walked into the living room to watch the news. But at the same time, I was sure I knew what it was.

"Oh…My…Goodness…" I said in a shocked voice.

"What?" asked Kate.

"Bella, you have the gift of telekinesis; you know where you can move things with your mind. Kate, the whole thing with the fire and the stove yesterday, I think you have the gift of fire. And Lynn, today first you were grumpy, then you were happy, then you were grumpy again, and now you're happy again, and today outside… I-I think you have the gift of weather," I answered.

"REALLY?!" Lynn and Kate cried excitedly.

"Oh, my goodness, this makes so much sense!" Bella cried.

"Doesn't it?!" I exclaimed.

"This is awesome! Now all of us have powers! Oh, sorry, Mary Ann," said Bella.

"It's okay," I replied. "All of you got your powers on different days, so maybe I'll get a power tomorrow."

My friends and I enjoyed watching each other play with our new powers throughout the day. Well, my friends didn't watch me because I didn't have a power…yet. When we played board games, Bella used her telekinesis to move her game piece. When we were outside, Lynn would use her weather powers to make small thunder clouds on the beach. Later that evening, we decided to make a campfire and cook s'mores; Kate used her fire powers to start the fire. All throughout the day, I was happy for my friends but disappointed that I didn't have my own powers to play with.

The next day, I waited, and waited, and waited for something to happen. Eventually, I decided to go for a swim and to clear my mind. My friends said they wanted to play with their powers and that I should go ahead, and they would be out in a little bit. So, I threw my swimsuit on, grabbed a towel, and went for a swim. I took a deep breath and dived down into the ocean. I was far enough from shore that my head was about five feet underwater. When I dove down, my foot got tangled in some old fishing line caught on an old tree trunk. I tried wiggling free, but it was no use. My foot was caught, and it wouldn't budge! The worst part was my head was underwater. I could drown if I were down here for over a minute. I started thinking fast; I also did something I always do when I'm thinking. I started twiddling my thumbs. I was thinking and twiddling, thinking, and twiddling, when I realized that the water around me was whirling. Whirling, circling around, faster and faster. Somehow the water got my foot free, and the water was pushing me up out of the ocean. Within seconds my head was out of the water, and I could breathe! The water pushed me up so high that I flew through the air, landing hard on my stomach in the sand! My friends came running over.

"Are you okay?" Kate asked.

"I think so," I answered.

"What just happened?" asked Lynn.

"I'm not entirely sure, but...I think I just found my power," I replied. I stood up, walked over toward the water, held my hand out, and a blob of water floated above the ocean. I slowly raised my hand and split the one giant water ball into two medium-sized water balls. I lowered the balls into the water and turned around to see three amazed and surprised faces.

"Now we all have powers!" exclaimed Bella. I was so excited, but then Lynn said, "Come, let's go show my Aunt Isabel." Lynn turned around and was about to run toward the house when I grabbed her arm and stopped her.

"Lynn, we can't tell Isabel," I said. "We can't tell anybody. Not friends, not family, not kids at school, not anybody!"

"Why not?" asked Bella.

"Because these powers are awesome, but they aren't normal. If kids at school found out, they would either think that we're the coolest people on earth or that we're freaks," I replied. At that moment, we suddenly didn't think our powers were extraordinary. Instead, we thought they were the worst things on earth.

The next morning my friends and I were heading home. The first thing I felt like doing once I woke up was staying in my bed forever. Even though I missed my family, I didn't want the vacation to end. But I forced myself to get out of bed anyway. I changed out of my pj's, brushed my teeth and hair, packed up all my stuff, and had breakfast. Then my friends and I brought our suitcases outside, where Isabel was waiting.

"Thanks for letting us stay, Aunt Isabel," said Lynn hugging her aunt.

"Thanks," the rest of us said.

"Oh, it was no biggie. I love seeing my Lynnie Bear and meeting my Lynnie Bear's friends," replied Isabel. A few seconds later, we all piled into Isabel's car, where she drove us to the dock, where we all got on the ferry to return home.

Chapter 5

Don't Tell

The trip home was kind of the same as before, just…a bit tenser. On the boat, the girls played "would you rather," and I watched. Then in the car with Lynn's mom, we did our best to avoid talking about the fact that we now had powers.

Then about thirty minutes later, the girls and I got home.

"All right, well, I'm going home. See you guys tomorrow. Also, good luck keeping the secret," I said with a whisper.

"Right back at ya," said Bella.

So, I went home, and a few minutes later, Kate, Lynn, and Bella also went home. I walked into my house, painted light mint green with light pink doors on the outside. Almost everybody in my family is an artist, just in our own different ways. For example, I like to draw and paint. My brother, Mark, likes to draw, and my other brother, Brian, likes writing songs, and then he plays them on his guitar. I don't have any sisters, only brothers.

So, it's me, my brother, Mark, my brother, Brian, my mom, and my dad. Once I got inside my house, I ran into my brothers.

"Hey, Mary Ann, how was your week at Lynn's Aunt's house?" asked Brian.

I froze. Since my brothers and I were so close, keeping the secret would be more challenging than I thought. After a minute or so, I finally replied.

"It was great! Nothing weird happened at all," I said as I giggled nervously.

"Umm, okay?" said Mark.

"So, umm, what did you guys do when I was gone?" I asked.

"Well, I worked on some more music while you were gone," said Brian.

"Cool. Can you play one of your songs for me?" I asked.

Brian replied, "Sure, let's go to my room, and I can play you a song." So, Brian, Mark, and I went down the hall to Brian's bedroom.

That evening I went upstairs to my bedroom. My room is big with white walls with little splashes of color. A little blue there, a little pink there, a little orange there, and you know all the colors in a rainbow. I also have paintings that I did myself hung up all over my walls. I even have a loft bed. (You know, one of those beds that has a desk underneath it.) So, I climbed into my bed, got my phone, and called Kate.

Once Kate picked up her phone, I said, "Did you know keeping the secret would be this hard?!? Once my brothers asked me, how was your week at Lynn's Aunt's? I froze!"

Kate replied, "No! I didn't know it would be so hard. Emily and I share everything with each other, and now I have a huge, and I mean HUGE, secret that I can't tell her! I texted her once I got home and almost told her!"

"KATE!" I yelled.

"I know. I know," Kate answered.

"Well, we have to do something," I said.

When Kate was about to say something, her little brother, Collin, walked into her room and said, "Kate, you read to me every night before I go to bed, and my bedtime is in 30 minutes."

"Okay, just give me a minute, and I'll read to you. I got to go. Peace out, Mary Ann," said Kate.

"Okay, talk to you later, bye," I said. I hung up the phone, and a few seconds later, I heard a door downstairs open and close. Then I got out of bed and went downstairs. When I got downstairs, I saw...

"DAD!" I said, running down the last few stairs to hug my dad.

"BELLA BEAR!" My dad said, grabbing me in a big bear hug.

(Bella Bear is the nickname my father gave me the day I was born. Bella is short for Isabella, which is my middle name.)

"How was your week at Lynn's Aunt's house?" My father asked.

I froze again. Of course, my dad wanted to know about my week at Isabel's house. I finally said, "It was great! Nothing weird happened at all." My dad had a confused look on his face.

Mark spoke up, "That's all she would tell us, too. She's very secretive about what happened."

I stood there for a minute, then said, "Lynn's Aunt Isabel's house was fun...nothing weird happened...yep...just a normal time... (I giggled nervously). We went to the beach, and Ummm...we just hung out."

"Okay, well, that's something," Dad said.

Not knowing what to do next, I said, "Well, l, umm, I'm going to go upstairs and do some drawing." Then, I turned around and went upstairs. Once I got into my room, I picked up my sketchbook and a pencil. I sat down, tired and hungry, at my desk and started drawing. After an hour of drawing, I went downstairs, got a snack, then went to bed.

The next morning, I was woken up by my phone. Kate was Face

Timing me. I picked up my phone and answered.

"I called you five times already; where were you?!?" Kate asked impatiently.

I replied, "I've been asleep in bed."

"Yeah, I can tell - nice bedhead," Kate said sarcastically.

I glared at my best friend and said sarcastically, "Ha-ha, very funny." Then, I looked at the clock on my bedroom wall, "Why are you calling me at 7:00 A.M. on a Saturday?"

"I just found out that my cousins, Emily and Blair, are coming over later today," said Kate.

I looked shocked and then replied, "What? No, we just got home from the island yesterday. You and Emily tell each other everything! You're not ready for that!"

"DUH! What am I going to do?" asked Kate.

"I don't know, umm, what if maybe I come over to your house and hang out with you guys and make sure that you…well, you don't let the cat out of the bag," I said, whispering that last part. Kate thought about it for a minute and knew it was a great idea.

After Kate hung up, I left my room, brushed my teeth and hair, went downstairs, and got breakfast.

"Good morning, sweetheart," My mom said when I walked into the kitchen.

I replied, "Morning, mom. Hey, is it okay if I go over to Kate's house today?"

"Umm, sure, I guess," My mom said as she poured a bowl of cereal for me.

"Thanks, mom," I said while taking the cereal from her.

Five minutes later, I said goodbye to my mom and headed to Kate's house after eating. Luckily, Kate's house is three minutes away. My friends and I live close to each other, so it doesn't take but a few minutes to walk to each other's houses. When walking from my house Kate lives three minutes away, Bella lives five minutes away, and Lynn lives seven minutes away.

About three, maybe four minutes later, I got to Kate's house. I rang the doorbell - ding dong. Not long after, Kate's little brother, Collin, another friend of mine, answered the door.

"Hi, Collin. Is Kate here?" I asked.

Collin smiled and replied, "Hey, Mary Ann. Yeah, Kate's here. Come on in. Did you know my cousins Emily and Blair are coming over?"

"Thanks, and so I heard. Did you get taller?" I said as I walked into the house.

Collin chuckled and said, "Yeah, I have."

"Cool," I said as I stood there clutching my purse.

Then, Kate said, "Oh, hey, Mary Ann. Collin, go feed Marshmallow."

"Okay," said Collin.

"Marshmallow?" I asked.

"Marshmallow is Collin's new baby bunny. We named him Marshmallow because he's white and fluffy," Kate explained.

"AAAWWW, baby bunny!" I said.

"Anyway, Emily and Blair will be here any minute. So, what do we do?" asked Kate.

"Chill, Kate, chill. As long as we stick to the plan, we'll be fine," I said calmly as I set my purse down on the table.

"What plan?" Collin asked as he walked into the room.

"Umm, the plan about Bella's surprise birthday party next month," I lied.

"Okay," said Collin.

After Collin entered the kitchen, Kate leaned over to me and whispered, "I can't believe that worked!"

I giggled and said, "I know, right."

All of a sudden, there was a knock at the door…

"That would be your cousins," I said.

"Let's do this," Kate said. Kate opened the door and said, "Hi, Emily. Hi, Blair. So good to see you."

"Hey, Kate. Great to see you, too," Emily said with a smile.

"Hello, Kate," said Blair.

"Come on in, you guys. You remember Mary Ann, right?" Kate asked.

"Yeah, hey, Mary Ann," replied Emily while giving Kate and me hugs. The girls and I talked for a while, and then Kate's mom got home.

"Hi, mom," said Collin.

Kate's mom replied, "Hi kids, mind helping me bring in the groceries?"

"Sure," we said.

After we were done helping, we went back to Kate's room to hang out. We chatted for a while about school and Emily's latest volleyball tournament. Then Emily asked, "Can we play truth or dare?"

"No! Not truth or dare! I always end up embarrassed or doing something I don't want to do," I complained.

Emily rolled her eyes and said, "Well, too bad. I dare you to go up to Kate's mom and yell…I LIKE BANANAS!" Then Emily started laughing her head off.

I rolled my eyes and said, "I'm out of here." Then I walked out of Kate's room and headed toward the door.

"I'll be right back," said Kate while she walked out of the room. "Mary Ann,wait, wait, wait, please stay. I need your help."

"Why do you need my help? We've been talking for an hour and a half, and you haven't done anything to show that we have powers," I said with a bit of anger in my voice.

"Yeah, I haven't yet. Who knows what will happen when you leave? Please?" asked Kate.

I stood there for a minute and said, "Okay, fine, I'll stay." So, Kate and I went back to Kate's room.

"Yay, you're back. Now go do your dare," said Emily pointing toward the door.

I sighed, turned around, and did my stupid dare while the others laughed like crazy. About an hour later, we had lunch, and I headed home. I told Kate to text me if something terrible happened - like if Kate accidentally almost told everyone that she had powers.

Chapter 6

Spending time with friends

Blair and Emily left the next morning. Then, Kate went to the playground across the street and texted Bella, Lynn, and me to meet her there.

"So, what happened with Emily and Blair?" Lynn had asked once we sat down on the swings.

"How did you know about them?" asked Kate.

"Mary Ann told us," Bella said with a smile and a giggle.

"Anyway, it was fine. It all went smoothly," said Kate.

I interrupted, "Yeah, until Emily made me scream 'I like bananas' in your mom's face, and I had to lock myself in your closet."

Lynn, Bella, and Kate burst out laughing.

"Oh yeah, that was funny," said Kate.

"No, it was not!" I said with an embarrassed expression on my face.

"Okay, okay, okay, let's stop laughing. Mary Ann looks embarrassed," said Lynn.

I got up from where I was sitting and walked away. Once Bella, Lynn,

and Kate caught their breath Bella said, "Wait, Mary Ann, come back."
I replied, "No! I'm doing what my mom said to do when I get mad at
someone. Just walk away."

Lynn, Bella, and Kate walked over to me and hugged me.

"We're sorry," said Bella.

"Fine. I forgive you guys," I said.

After a couple of minutes, Lynn asked, "So, what did Kate's mom do
once you screamed 'I like bananas' in her face?"

I chuckled and said, "Don't even start with me."

The next day when I got home, I started writing in my diary.

> Dear Diary,
> A few days ago, I got home from my week at Lynn's
> aunt's house with Kate, Lynn, and Bella. You'll never
> believe what happened there. My friends and I went
> for a hike, and we found this cool cave with a weird
> blueish-green light coming from it. We got lost when
> we were in there, and after about ten minutes, we saw
> a light coming from the outside but the floor. We all
> looked down, and there was a pool filled with pinkish-
> purple water with glass covering the top of it where
> we were standing. We screamed, the glass broke, and
> we fell in. We didn't know what had happened to us
> until the following day. Bella, Kate, Lynn, and I got
> powers! Bella was the first one to know that she had
> powers. Bella can move things with her mind. Then,
> Kate got her powers - she can control fire. Shortly after,
> Lynn got the power of weather. It took a while for me
> to get powers, but I got the power of water. I can control
> water and make water out of thin air. Anyway, Brian and
> Mark are calling my name. I better talk to you later—peace out.

"Oh, hey, there you are. Brian, she's in here!" said Mark as he walked
into my bedroom.

"Here I am," I replied with a giggle. A few seconds later, Brian walked into my bedroom.

"Hey, what are you doing?" Asked Brian.

"Oh, nothing," I said, trying to hide my diary from my brothers.

"What did you just hide under your pillow?" Asked Mark with a curious look on his face.

"Nothing," I had said quickly. Brian walked over to my bed, climbed on top of my loft bed, and quickly pulled my diary from under the pillows.

"You have a secret diary and didn't tell us?" Brian asked with a shocked look.

I had a sheepish look on my face and said, "I wouldn't call it a super secret."

Brian got down off my bed and ran out of my room. A few seconds later, Mark followed as I got down from my bed and yelled, "Brian, Mark, give it back!"

"Sorry, little sis, not until we read your secrets," said Brian. Then, I started to run faster. Finally, after a few more minutes of chasing Brian and Mark, Lynn walked in.

"What's going on here?" Lynn asked.

"They stole my diary and won't give it back!" I yelled. Lynn sighed, put down her backpack (which was pink and purple with little dogs on it), and helped me get my diary back. Eventually, I did get my diary back, but it took a little while.

"What is wrong with you, stealing Mary Ann's diary like that?" yelled Lynn.

I picked up Lynn's backpack and said, "Come on, Lynn, let's go upstairs." I glared at my brothers as I said those last few words.

Once Lynn and I got upstairs, and into my bedroom, Lynn said, "Dude, what was that? You and your brothers never fight."

"I know, but they just went for it once Brian and Mark saw my diary. I don't know why," I said, confused.

Lynn thought for a minute and then asked, "Have Brian and Mark ever seen your diary before?"

"No," I replied.

"Maybe your brothers wanted to know your secrets," Lynn thought out loud.

"Maybe. Anyway, why'd you pop over?" I asked.

Lynn sat down next to me and said, "My older sister, Hayley, was driving me nuts, so I went to Bella's house to see if she wanted to go out for ice cream, but her little brother, Luke, was taking a nap. Her mom and dad are not home, so she can't go anywhere. So then, I went over to Kate's house, but her mom said that Kate was taking a nap. So then, I was coming over here to see if you were busy, and yeah."

Then I said with a giggle, "Oh, wow! Thanks for making me your last choice."

"Sorry," Lynn replied with a sheepish look on her face.

I punched Lynn's shoulder playfully and said, "So you said something about ice cream?" We ended our weekend by getting ice cream together.

Chapter 7

Gina's a Meanie

Beep, beep, beep, beep, went Bella's alarm clock on Monday morning. Bella groaned, turned off her alarm clock, and sat up.

"In a way, I kind of forgot how awful it is to wake up at 6:00 in the morning," Bella said out loud to herself. Then, Bella jumped out of bed and went to the bathroom to brush her teeth and hair.

"Good morning, Mom; good morning, Luke," said Bella as she walked into the kitchen.

Luke turned around and said, "Morning, Bella."

"Good morning, B," Bella's mom replied. Bella hugged her mom and her little brother and then got some breakfast. Once Bella finished her breakfast, she got her backpack together and went outside to wait for the bus. Once the bus pulled up, Bella got on the bus and sat down next to me.

"Bella, you made it! We thought you might miss the bus and be late for school," I said with a chuckle.

Bella chuckled and said, "Nope, not today."

About forty-five minutes later, my friends and I got to school and ran into Noah.

"Oh hey, Noah," said Kate. Noah is a friend of mine and Kate, Lynn, and Bella, of course. Like Lynn, Noah has light brown hair and dark brown eyes like Kate.

Noah smiled and said, "Haven't seen you, girls, in a while. How was your summer?"

I rolled my eyes and said, "Oh you! It was only Spring Break, and you know that."

"Yeah, but Spring Break lasts for what feels like forever," said Noah.

"It was a week, and you know it," said Kate, crossing her arms and staring at Noah. Then the bell for class rang.

"Whatever. I got to get to class. So peace out, y'all," said Noah.

"Later, Noah," My friends and I said almost simultaneously.

"I better get to class, too. See you later," I said as I started walking away.

Two hours later, it was lunchtime. Before lunch, I stopped off at my locker to put my math books away, but while I was putting my books away, someone started talking to me.

"Well, well, well," a girl's voice said.

At first, I couldn't place the voice, but once I closed my locker, I saw Gina. Gina's the mean girl at the school. You know, that girl who's always making fun of you? But the weird part is that Gina didn't pick on anybody else, just me. No one ever knew why. Gina has red hair and sparkling bluebell eyes. She had on a beautiful purple dress with sparkles. Her shoes had heels that were at least two inches high, making her about a foot taller than me.

"What do you want, Gina?" I asked.

Gina laughed. "Silly little Mary Ann, I don't want anything," said Gina.

I looked confused and asked, "You don't?"

Gina smiled and said, "No. But there is something I need. I know that boys at this school think you're cute."

"What? No, they don't," I said with a shocked look.

Gina glared at me and replied, "Oh no? How many love notes did you get in your locker last Valentine's Day?"

"Twenty. But that doesn't mean anything!" I said with a bit of anger in my voice.

Gina was obviously furious with me, but then she took a deep breath and said calmly, "Look, Mary Ann, like I said, I don't want anything, but I need you to stay away from Shawn. Okay?"

"Shawn? Shawn Jones? The boy that most girls in this school want to go out with, Shawn?!" I said, still with a confused look on my face.

Gina rolled her eyes and nodded her head.

"Are you saying that you think I want to date Shawn? I don't want to date Shawn. I don't even think he knows I'm alive," I said, panicked.

"Just stay away from him, and if you don't, I will hurt you!" Gina practically yelled. Then Gina started walking away but stopped and rammed me into my locker. I turned around and watched Gina walk away while thinking about what she might do to me. That's when I saw Lynn. Thankfully Lynn's locker was just across the hall. So Lynn walked over to me.

"Did you hear that?" I asked.

"Yeah, I did. Are you okay?" asked Lynn as she put her arm around my shoulder. I looked back to where Gina had exited and nodded my head.

"Come on, let's go get some lunch," said Lynn, as she grabbed my hand and walked to the cafeteria. So Lynn and I ate our lunch and sat next to Kate and Bella.

"Mary Ann, just ignore her. Gina's just full of hot air," Lynn said as we sat down.

"What are you talking about?" asked Kate.

"A few minutes ago, Gina said that she would hurt Mary Ann if she didn't stay away from Shawn," replied Lynn.

Bella looked shocked, and then she looked confused and then asked, "Shawn? Shawn Jones? The boy that a bunch of girls wants to date, Shawn? You don't want to date Shawn. Does Shawn even know you're alive?"

"Yep, that's pretty much what I said," I said, looking down at my plate, clearly too distracted to eat.

"It'll be fine. All you need to do is to stay away from Shawn," said Kate with a mouth full of food.

I looked up from my food and said, "And how exactly do I stay away from him? We're in History, Math, English, and French together!" I scoffed and slammed my head into the table. Lynn placed her hand on my back and tried to make me feel better.

Kate had an angry look on her face and then stood up and said, "Okay, that's it! I'm talking to Gina." Kate walked up to Gina and told her, "Hey, Gina, look, you can't make Mary Ann stay away from Shawn."

Gina crossed her arms and asked, "Oh yeah, and why not?"

"Because you said she can't be around Shawn, even though they have four classes together," said Kate.

"Well, you and Mary Ann can get over it," said Gina as she walked away. Kate glared at Gina as she walked away and returned to the table.

"Well, I tried," said Kate as she sat down.

"What?!? You were talking for like three minutes," I said.

"Don't worry, Mary Ann. I'm sure we'll figure out something. Now eat. You'll need food in you for the next four hours," said Bella.

Thirty minutes later, lunch was over, and my friends and I went to class.

"Come on, Mary Ann, let's get to French class, and don't worry, I'll be there. There's no way that Gina can harm you when I'm around," said Bella as she closed her locker, grabbed my arm, and walked to class.

Once class started, the French teacher, Mr. Blake, said, "Today, you will be paired up with another kid to practice your French. Now, I will tell you who will be paired up with whom. Let's see Kelsie, John, and Henry; Alex, Kim, and Becky; Bella and Hannah; Mary Ann and Shawn." Bella and I looked at each other with horrified looks on our faces.

Then, Bella raised her hand, stood up, and said, "Umm, Mr. Blake, I think Mary Ann and I should be together. After all, we have known each other since we were nine, and we get along well."

Mr. Blake thought about it for a minute, then said, "Okay, then new plan. It'll be Bella and Mary Ann and Shawn and Hannah." Bella and I both had relieved looks on our faces. A few hours later school was over, and my friends and I met at Kate's locker.

"Hey, girls, how did French class go, you know, with Shawn and everything?" asked Kate.

I set my teal backpack with little unicorn doughnuts on it and then said, "When Mr. Blake said that Shawn and I were going to work together to practice our French, it was bad. But, thankfully, Bella spoke up and said that me and Bella…"

"Bella and I," interrupted Lynn.

I rolled my eyes and continued, "Anyway. When Bella said that BELLA AND I should be together instead, Mr. Blake agreed," I said. Kate chuckled.

"Hey, what are you laughing about?" asked Lynn.

"Yeah. Do you even know what Gina would do to me if Gina found out if Shawn and I were practicing together? She would kill me!" I said with a slight giggle.

"I know, right?!?" said Kate. At this point, all four of us were laughing our heads off.

Once Lynn caught her breath she asked, "Everybody else is going outside to wait for the bus. Do you guys want to go outside, too?"

"Good timing, Lynn. Brian just texted me and said I need to get home in about an hour to finish getting ready for friends and family movie and game night. Oh, and that reminds me, you guys coming over for that?" I asked while sending Brian a text (Saying, kay, kay, about to get on the bus now.)

"Wouldn't miss it for the world," replied Kate.

"I'll be there, too," said Lynn.

"You know it," said Bella with a smile.

So, the girls and I went outside and got on the bus shortly after.

Chapter 8

Friends and Family Night

"I'm home," I yelled as I walked through the door.

"Oh, hey sis, glad you're back. We need to finish cleaning the house before company tonight," said Mark.

I picked up some books from the table and said, "Okay. Since my room is always clean, all I need to do is pick up stuff around the house."

"Oh, yeah, I was trying to put some stuff away in your room, and since I have no idea where everything goes in your room, some stuff got messed up," said Mark with a shrug like it wasn't important. Then, without saying another word, I dashed up to my room. There were books, dresses, stuffed animals, and paintings that I painted myself all over the floor, along with a messy bed I had made just that morning.

MARK!" I yelled. My brother walked up to me and said, "Look, I know it's bad, but…"

I interrupted angrily, "BAD?! WHEN I LEFT FOR SCHOOL THIS MORNING, MY BEDROOM WAS SPOTLESS, AND NOW LOOK AT IT! IT WILL TAKE ME ALL DAY TO CLEAN MY ROOM IF OUR FRIENDS ARE COMING BY 8:OO P.M.!!"

Mark's face had a sheepish expression, and he said, "Oh, umm, you didn't hear? They aren't coming at 8:00; they're coming at 6:00." A terrified look spread across my face; I spun my head toward the clock on my wall; it read 3:30.

"Two and a half hours?" I said right before I started running around my room, trying to clean it as fast as possible.

"Okay, well, if you don't need me anymore, I'm going to go back downstairs and help Brian," said Mark as he walked off. But I wasn't paying attention and kept cleaning. Two hours later, I was still cleaning my room, and my brothers were downstairs cleaning when Brian said, "Mary Ann has been up there for a while; I'm going to go check on her." Brian handed Mark the broom and went upstairs to my bedroom. Knock…knock…knock…

"Hi, Brian," I said as I opened my bedroom door.

"Hey, Mary Ann, everything good up here?" My brother asked me to look at my room while peeking over my shoulder. I nodded my head and stepped aside to let him have a better look.

"Wow, this looks good, considering you've been working on it for the past two hours," Brian said, looking around my room. My eyes got wide.

"THE PAST TWO HOURS!" I screamed. I looked at the clock on my wall. Brian was right; it had been two hours.

"Um, okay, it's fine. I just need to put a few more things away and get ready. You and Mark should get ready too," I said.

"Okay, I'll do that now. See you later, Mary Ann," said Brian as he walked down the hall.

I closed my bedroom door put a couple of books away, changed into my pajamas, got some board games and card games out of my closet, and went downstairs to set out some snacks. I placed the games on the kitchen table and got out three glass bowls, filled one with chocolate-covered strawberries that I had made the day before, another bowl with raspberries, and the last bowl with blueberries. I also got out a glass plate on which I had placed cheese and crackers and other glass dishes I had set candy in, like jellybeans, suckers, and much more. Not long after, the guests started arriving. The first to arrive were my friends.   Then Mark's friend Ethan came, then Brian's friends Joel and Matt. Finally, everybody was dressed in their PJs and ready to have a fun night.

About twenty minutes later, after a little get-to-know-you circle, like we always do at friends and family night, my friends and I were in my room playing a little game called "How Many Ways Can You Use Your Powers." At the same time, my brothers and their friends watched television. I grabbed four cups from the cabinet and headed upstairs with my friends. We sat down in a circle on the floor, and I handed each of my friends a cup.

"What are these for?" Kate asked, grabbing the cup that I was handing to her.

"We're going to play a little game called 'How Many Ways Can You Use Your Powers,'" I replied.

"Awesome," said Bella and Lynn at the same time. I closed my eyes waved my hands in the air, and made four tiny water bubbles in the air. Then, I lowered my hands to the ground, and the water bubbles splashed into the cups. My friends applauded me.

"Me next!" said Lynn. Lynn stood up, waved her arms in the air, and made a little cloud right in the middle of my room, then Lynn moved her hands toward the cloud, and it started raining in my room. Kate, Bella, and I jumped up, trying not to get wet.

"Oops," said Lynn. She made the rainy cloud disappear, and Kate put her hand out and used her fire powers. She, in a way, set her hand on fire, then lowered her hand to the ground making the water on my carpet evaporate. Once she was done, I got on one knee and felt the carpet below my feet.

"The carpet isn't wet anymore! Thanks, Kate!" I said as I stood up and hugged Kate.

"Well, that's one way Kate can use her powers," said Bella. Kate looked thoughtful, then asked me, "Do you guys have any candles somewhere?"

"Yeah, in the closet downstairs; why?" I asked. Without saying another word, Kate dashed downstairs and ran back into my room a few minutes later, with one candle in each hand. She sat back next to me, set the candles on the floor, and used her powers to light the candles. Lynn, Bella, and I applauded her.

"My turn!" Bella said excitedly as she stood up. Bella held her hand toward my desk (it looked like she was trying to use force); using her powers, she made a piece of paper and a pencil float toward us. After about an hour of playing games and using our powers, Brian called my friend's names from downstairs. "KATE, BELLA, LYNN, YOUR PARENTS ARE HERE TO PICK YOU UP!"

"Has it been two hours already?" asked Bella.

"I guess so," I said. My friends and I walked downstairs, and I said goodbye to them. Shortly after, Ethan and Joel went home, too, but Matt stayed and spent the night.

Chapter 9

The Good News and the Bad News

The next morning, I woke up wishing that the night before had lasted forever. Brian's friend, Matt, who had spent the night at my house, saw me and said, "Good morning, Mary Ann."

"Good morning, Matt," I replied as I walked downstairs and into the kitchen.

Then, my brother, Brian, walked into the kitchen, yawned, and said, "Morning, Matt. Morning, Mary."

"Morning, Brian," I replied.

"What are you guys talking about?" Brian asked.

"Nothing," I replied. I got breakfast. I had toast with strawberry jam spread out on it and some scrambled eggs for breakfast. "I better go get ready for school; see you guys later," I said to my brother and his friend as I went back upstairs to get ready.

After I changed into a blue sweater, some jeans, and my white sandals, I got a text from Kate saying, "Are you ready for another painful day at school?"

I replied, "It won't be painful, LOL!"

"It will if Gina sees you near Shawn," Kate replied. I told Kate I had to go. After all, I can't waste time on a school morning talking to Kate. While I was getting ready, I couldn't stop thinking about what Kate had texted, "It will be if Gina sees you near Shawn." I knew Gina was out to get me. I packed an extra bag and filled it with stuff like band-aids, a few pills for headache reasons, and some makeup just in case Gina gave me a black eye, and I wanted to hide it from my brothers. After a while, I said goodbye to Brian and Mark and went outside to wait for the bus. Once I got on the bus, I only saw Lynn. So, I assumed Bella and Kate hadn't been picked up yet.

"Hey," I said to Lynn as I sat next to her.

"Hey, Mary Ann, feeling ready for today?" Lynn asked.

"You know it," I replied. A few minutes later, the bus driver picked up Bella and Kate, and we got to school thirty minutes later. Since my friends and I got our powers, we knew our lives would be different, and hard to hide our powers. But now I was dealing with my powers and the whole Gina and Shawn problem. My first few classes went by in a flash, and before I knew it, it was lunchtime.

"Are you okay, Mary Ann?" asked Bella once we sat down.

"Yeah, I'm fine. I am just a little nervous about the whole Gina thing," I replied.

"Mary Ann, stop worrying. It's not like Gina can do anything to you," said Kate.

"And if she tries to harm you, Kate, Bella, and I will always be by your side to help you," Lynn said, trying to comfort me.

There were a few minutes of silence, then Bella, who changed the topic, asked, "What do you think would happen if someone found out about our powers?"

Lynn and I looked at each other and said, "Brian and Mark would have if they had actually read my diary and not just taken it."

"Whoa, whoa, whoa, hold on. What?" asked Kate.

Lynn continued for me, "Remember on Sunday when I went to your homes to see if you guys were busy?" Kate and Bella nodded, and Lynn continued, "Well, when I went to Mary Ann's house, I walked in on her chasing her brothers because they stole her diary. Mary Ann told me that she wrote in her diary about our powers, and if her brothers read her diary, they would have found out."

"Mary Ann Isabella Sherman!" Kate whispered angrily.

"What were you expecting? If I have a secret, I need to tell someone or something, or else I go bananas, and there is no need for full names, Kathrin Elisabeth Tanner," I replied. Kate rolled her eyes. The rest of the day flew by, and I headed home.

A few minutes before I got home, I got a text from Brian," Are you on your way home yet?"

"Be home in five," I replied. When I got home, I saw my brothers playing video games in the family room.

"Hey, Mary Ann! Did you have a good day at school?" Mark asked me, taking his eyes off the screen for a split second to glance at me.

"Yeah, it was fine," I replied. After I got a snack, I realized I was exhausted, so I took a nap.

An hour later, I was awakened by a loud scream, "MARY ANN!!" I quickly sat up in my bed, startled. I ran downstairs and into the kitchen.

"MARK! MARK! WHAT'S THE MATTER?!" I asked.

"Where did you put the cupcakes you made yesterday?" asked Mark.

I rolled my eyes. "You woke me up for cupcakes?" I asked, filled with rage at my brother.

"Yep!" said Mark, clearly not picking up on my rage.

"Cupcakes are in the cabinet," I said, not caring anymore. Just then, I heard a jingle from my phone. "Oh, Lynn's Face Timing me. I'll be in my room if you need me," I yelled to Mark as I ran upstairs.

Once I answered the call, Lynn said, "Hi! I'm bored; why do you have bedhead? Oh, my goodness, did I wake you up from your nap? I'm so sorry!" (Lynn could be a little talkative sometimes.)

I replied, "No, you didn't wake me up. Mark woke me up because he couldn't find the cupcakes."

Lynn giggled and then asked, "Are you doing anything?"

I shook my head and said, "No, why?"

"No reason, just curious," Lynn replied. After about twenty more minutes of talking on the phone, I had to go because my dad got home early.

"Hi, dad!" I said as I walked downstairs to hug my dad.

"Hey, Mary Berry!" (Mary Berry is another one of my dad's nicknames he gave me.) "Is your mom home yet?" my dad asked.

"No, why?" Asked Brian as he entered the room.

"Because I have some big news I want to share with everybody," my dad replied. My brothers and I looked at each other and shrugged. Twenty minutes later, my mom came home and had some news too! My mom and dad both worked, and they both worked for a toy company! This is why my parents always ask my brothers and me about toy ideas. After a few minutes, my mom and dad sat Brian, Mark, and me down to share their news. My mom went first. "Kids I have some news, and it's not very good news. Today at work, I talked to my boss, and…he fired me," my mom said sadly.

"You got fired?" Mark echoed. My mom nodded her head. Then, my dad said, "That's okay because today I got a promotion. I'm now the vice-president. That means I'll be paid even more!"

"That's good," I said. After a while, I went to bed, figuring out if I should be really happy or worried about my parents' jobs. But all I wanted to do was fall asleep.

Chapter 10

Gina's a spy

The next morning, I woke up thirsty and had mixed feelings about what I had heard the night before. Luckily, I had an empty cup in my room. Using my water powers, I hovered my hand over the cup. I waved my hand in circles, and water splashed into my cup out of nowhere. Then, I drank it.

After changing into a t-shirt with a couple of kittens on it, dark blue jeans, and sneakers, I put my hair up in a French braid, ate breakfast, and brushed my teeth. Then, I ran downstairs, said goodbye to Brian and Mark, grabbed my unicorn backpack, and went outside to wait for the bus.

"Hey, Mary Ann, you ready for school today?" asked Kate. I chuckled, nodded my head, and sat down next to Bella. Then, after picking up a few more kids, we got to school.

"Do you guys think that we're ever going to use our powers at school?" asked Kate with a whisper. Lynn and Bella shrugged. Then Lynn noticed that I was not paying attention whatsoever.

"You okay, Mary Ann?" Lynn asked.

"Huh? Oh right, yeah, I'm fine, I guess. I just can't wrap my head around something," I replied.

"What's wrong?" Bella asked me as we stopped off at her locker. I looked down at my feet, then raised my head to look at my friends and said, "My mom got fired from her job." My friends looked shocked.

Kate responded with great concern in her voice, "What!"

"You're joking, right?" asked Lynn.

"Oh, my goodness," said Bella.

"Yep. Now my mom is home alone trying to find things to do," I replied. Then, the bell rang. "Oh, there's the bell. See you guys later," I said as I ran off.

The first classes flew by, and I hoped the rest of the day would be the same as the bell rang announcing that my history class was over and it was time for lunch. The voice inside my head went, "YAY! LUNCHTIME!" But I also knew that I had to use decorum. Decorum means being respectful and not yelling, "YAY, CLASS IS OVER!" once the bell rings. So I gathered my books, grabbed my backpack, and went to put my books in my locker before lunch.

As I was walking to lunch, I got a text from Kate saying, "Hey, Mary Ann, where are you? It's lunchtime."

I replied, "Be there in a minute; I had to put books in my locker." Once I got lunch and sat down next to my friends, I asked, "Anything exciting happening with you guys today?"

"Nope," replied Lynn.

"No, not really," said Kate.

"No. Why?" asked Bella.

"I don't know. I was just trying to make a conversion." Then, as my friends and I sat there eating our lunch in silence, not knowing what to talk about, we heard screaming from the kitchen.

"HELP! HELP! FIRE! FIRE!" The voices yelled. Then, the fire alarm rang, and all the students hurried outside. As my friends and I started walking toward the emergency exit, Kate pulled Lynn, Bella, and me into the hallway so that no one could see or hear us.

"What are you doing? We need to go outside," I said.

"Mary Ann, don't you see? There's a fire!" Kate said excitedly.

Lynn and I looked confused, but Bella caught on to what Kate was saying.

"Oh, I get it. There's a fire, and Mary Ann has water powers!" said Bella.

"Oh, right! Mary Ann, you can put out the fire!" Lynn said.

"No, I-I don't think so," I said. Little did we know that Gina was right around the corner listening to us. I thought about it for a minute and said, "You know what? I'll do it. I'll try to put out the fire."

We started running toward the cafeteria, and I guess Gina heard us running and started running that way too. My friends and I burst through the cafeteria's kitchen doors behind the counter. After we got into the kitchen, Gina very, very, quietly went through the kitchen doors, hid so that she couldn't be seen, pulled out her phone, and started filming me putting out the fire.

I took a deep breath, stuck out my hands, and waved them around in the air. Then, I formed a huge water blob and dropped it on top of the fire to put it out.

"I did it! I put out the fire!" I said excitedly.

"Yeah, you did! Let's go outside before anybody finds us, and we get in trouble," said Kate. So then, the five of us (including Gina, who we still didn't know was there) ran out of the cafeteria and outside and ensured no one saw us. Then, the firefighters got there to put out the fire, but they realized it had already been put out.

"Ma'am, I don't see any fire in that school," one of the firemen said to the cooks. Many students heard what the fireman had said and were all upset that their lunch had been interrupted.

"OKAY, KIDS, BACK IN THE BUILDING, FINISH YOUR LUNCH, THEN GET TO YOUR NEXT CLASS!" So announced one of the teachers.

After I finished my lunch, I went to my locker to get my notebook before French class. As I closed my locker door, I saw Gina. I sighed.

"What do you want, Gina?" I asked.

"Oh, Mary Ann, I don't want anything," said Gina with a laugh.

"That's what you said when you told me I need to stay away from Shawn," I replied.

Gina rolled her eyes and pulled me aside so no one could hear us. "Look, Mary Ann, I saw you were using your freaky powers, and if you go anywhere near Shawn, I'll show the video to everybody in the school," Gina said before she started walking away. I grabbed my phone out of my purse and texted my friends.

"Guys! We need to talk, but no time now; meet me at the park after school." I texted.

Then the bell rang. I had to get to French class. After French class, I only had two classes left; English and art class. Before I knew it school was over. Once the final bell rang, I gathered my pad of paper and pencils and walked out of the classroom with decorum, but after I was out of eyesight, I ran as fast as possible to get to the park. Right before I reached the school doors, I ran into Shawn Jones. Not only did I run into him…I tripped and fell.

"Are you okay?" Shawn asked as he held his hand out to help me up. I stood up with a voice inside my head that was panicking about how I ran into Shawn.

"Yes, I'm fine! Sorry, I got to go!" I said as I ran away. Now I had two things to worry about; Gina knowing that I have powers and the possibility that Gina might have seen me talking to Shawn. But at the moment, all I needed to do was get to the park to talk to my friends.

Chapter 11

The Note

I was at the park for about ten minutes before my friends arrived. Then, I saw Kate, Bella, and Lynn, come running up to me.

"Mary Ann, what's the emergency?" Kate asked, out of breath.

"Gina knows about our powers! While we were in the kitchen, she was recording us!" I replied.

"What?! How did we not see or hear her?" asked Lynn.

"Who cares?! What will Gina do with the video?" asked Bella.

"Gina said she would show the whole school the video if I got anywhere near Shawn. So when I was leaving school, I ran into Shawn! Literally!" I replied.

"Oh, no! Did Gina see you?" asked Lynn.

"I don't think so, but she might have," I replied.

"What will we do if Gina tells the whole school we have powers?" Bella asked.

Before anybody could answer Bella's question, Kate asked, "Why do we need to keep our powers a secret? I mean, if Gina will tell the whole school, anyway?"

No one answered Kate's question... So why did we have to keep it a secret?

"Because we don't want people to think that we're freaks with freaky powers?" said Lynn questioningly.

Then Kate's phone buzzed. "Oh, it's a text from my mom. Let me see what it says" "Hey, Kate! Have you picked Collin up yet?" Kate texted her mom, "No, I'll do that now."

"Well, I got to pick my brother up at the bus stop. See you guys later," said Kate, right before she started running toward the bus stop.

"I should get home, too. I just remembered that I have to look after Luke this afternoon. Bye guys!" said Bella before she started walking toward her house.

"Do you need to leave, too?" Lynn asked me.

I shook my head and said, "Nope, I've got nothing to do for the rest of the day. What about you?"

Lynn shook her head.

"Want to hang out for a while?" I asked.

"Sure, let me just text my mom and let her know I'll be home later," Lynn replied.

"Okay, I'll let my brothers know, too," I said. So then Lynn and I hung out for about an hour, then Lynn went home, and I went home, too. After I got to my house, I got a text from Gina. The text said, "I saw you with Shawn today. You will be sorry." Then Gina sent me the video she took of me with my powers and said, "At lunch, on Monday, everybody in the school will see this video." I read the text as I walked into the kitchen.

"Oh no, this is bad," I said out loud.

"What's wrong, Mary Ann?" asked Brian. I looked up, realizing that my brothers were in the room.

"Um, I just got a text from my Math teacher; I have three tests I need to study for by Monday," I lied.

"Three?" asked Mark suspiciously.

"Yep! Anyway, I better go study, bye!" I said as I started walking toward the stairs. Brian quickly grabbed my phone from my hand, and my brothers read the texts from Gina.

"HEY! Give me my phone!" I said. Then Brian and Mark watched the video and were shocked.

"Mary, what is this?" asked Brian.

"Look, I know it looks bad, but," before I could finish my sentence Mark cut in.

"Bad?! It's awesome! How long have you had powers?"

"Since Spring Break," I replied, calming down a bit.

"Wait…you mean, at Lynn's Aunt's house? Why didn't you tell anyone? I get that mom and dad might freak out, but you could have told us. But as far as the powers go, sis, that's awesome! Do your friends have powers, too?" Brian asked, interested.

"Wait, is mom home?" I asked to make sure she wouldn't hear us. Mark replied, "No, she went to the gym." So I sat down and answered Brian's question.

"Yes, my friends have powers. For example, Kate can control fire, Lynn can control the weather, and Bella can move things with her mind."

"That's so cool," said Mark.

"Wait is this why when you got home from your trip you were all like, 'It was great! Nothing weird happened at all!'?" asked Brian.

"Yeah, it was tough to keep it a secret at first," I said. My brothers and I talked about my powers for about ten more minutes. Then our mom got home.

"Hi, mom!" I said cheerfully.

"Hi, kids!" my mom replied. I yawned.

"I'm going to go upstairs and take a nap," I said as I grabbed my phone from Brian and rushed upstairs. While napping, I dreamt I could breathe underwater. I also dreamt that I went for a swim in the ocean and danced with a dolphin. About an hour later, I was woken up by the doorbell. I got up and quickly brushed my hair to get the tangles out because I usually wake up with bedhead. Once I got to the door, I looked through the window to see who it was, but nobody was there. I opened the door, and there was nobody in sight other than the next-door neighbors jumping on their trampoline. I closed the door.

"Who was there?" asked Mark.

"There was nobody there," I replied. The doorbell rang again. I opened the door yet again. There was no one there, just a card on the welcome mat. I picked up the note and read it out loud as Brian entered the room. The note said,

"I saw you near Shawn today, and I thought I couldn't make you stay away from Shawn. So, I won't make you. JUST KIDDING! You will pay for what you did today. I will ensure you will never want to show your face again. Punches and kisses, Gina!"

"Yikes! That's harsh. Hey, Mary, who's Shawn?" Brian asked me.

"Shawn Jones is this guy at my school. About half the girls at school want to date him, and a bunch of the boys at school wants to go out with me! Last Valentine's Day, I got over twenty love notes in my locker. Three of them were from the same guy. Anyway, Gina's convinced that since a bunch of other guys like me, Shawn might. So, she said that if I got anywhere near him, she would kill me! So, I've been trying to avoid him, and when I left school today, I ran into him. Literally,"

"That is not okay. Nobody threatens my baby sister!" Mark said angrily.

"Mark, I'm thirteen. I'm not a baby," I replied.

"It doesn't matter; on Monday, I'm going to talk to Gina and set her straight!" said Brian.

"No, you guys! I don't want Gina to think I need my big brothers to stand up for me. I'm a teenager and need to learn to stand on my own two feet. Okay, I'm sorry, but I don't need my brothers to stand up for me all the time," I replied. Mark started to say something as I walked toward the stairs, but Brian stopped him.

"Mark, let her go. I'm proud of her," Brian said as he put his hand out to stop his brother. Brian decided that I could handle Gina on my own, but Mark was slightly more protective of me and wasn't convinced.

The weekend dragged because I knew what was coming on Monday. As I was getting ready for school, I was so nervous. I knew that by the end of the day, everybody in the school would know about my powers and, of course, my friends' powers. But then I had something else to think about because out of the corner of my eye; I saw Mark march right up to Gina.

"Hey, you, Gina?" Mark asked sternly.

"That's me. You've heard of me?" Gina replied just as sternly.

"Yeah, I have. From Mary Ann, my baby sister," said Mark as he glared at Gina, filling up with rage. Gina chuckled softly. I ran over to the two of them and angrily whispered, "Mark! What are you doing here?"

"Mark just told me how much he loves his sweet baby sister!" Gina said with a babyish voice and rubbed the top of my head as if I was a puppy.

"I CAN'T BELIEVE YOU! I DIRECTLY SAID TO YOU AND BRIAN I AM A TEENAGER AND CAN STAND ON MY OWN TWO FEET!" By then, everyone in the hallway was staring at me while yelling at my brother, "MARK, I'M NOT FIVE, ANYMORE! SO, I DON'T NEED YOU TO ALWAYS BE BY MY SIDE TO MAKE ME FEEL BETTER WHEN I FALL OFF THE MONKEY BARS AT THE PARK OR TO STAY HOME WITH ME WHEN MOM AND DAD AREN'T HOME! OKAY, I'M GROWING UP, AND SO ARE YOU! SO, YOU NEED TO ACT LIKE IT!" I stopped, realizing that I had gone too far.

"Fine. Sorry for trying to make sure that my only sister is okay and safe," Mark replied, clearly hurt by my words. I stared at Mark as he walked off. Finally, I walked back to my friends and said, "I went too far."

"No, yeah," replied Kate.

"Ok. I'll apologize to him tonight," I said with a sigh.

Chapter 12

The Mighty Gina Has Been Slain

"You okay, Mary Ann?" asked Bella.

"Huh? Oh, oh yeah, I'm great. It's just Gina's planning to show the whole school the video of us. It's just making me a nervous wreck." I said,

"Oh, that's right. By the end of the day, the secret will be out," Lynn said, looking out into space.

"What if the secret was out, but people didn't know it?" Kate said half to herself.

"What are you talking about?" I asked, really confused. Kate continued, "I have an idea that ensures that Gina won't be able to tell anyone about our powers." We got closer together, so no one could hear us. Bella, Lynn, and I agreed it was a good idea. A few hours later, at lunch, before my friends and I could even get our food, we got everybody's attention.

"ATTENTION, LADIES, AND GENTLEMEN! MY FRIENDS AND I HAVE SOMETHING TO SHOW YOU!" Kate announced loudly to the whole room. "WE MADE A LITTLE SHORT MOVIE THAT IS SO COOL! THE MOVIE IS ABOUT ME AND MY FRIENDS HERE - MARY ANN, BELLA, AND LYNN. IN THE MOVIE WE HAVE POWERS!" I could see Gina looking straight up at us with a shocked face. Then, Kate pressed a button, and the video started; just like Kate said, the secret was out, but nobody knew. A few minutes later, the video had ended, and Gina walked up to me.

"You were smart, showing everyone the video and telling them that you made a movie. But this doesn't mean I'll stop threatening you to stay away from Shawn," Gina said, pointing her finger at me.

"I know," I said, lowering Gina's finger.

Without saying another word, Gina walked away. Knowing lunch would be over within thirty minutes, my friends and I got our food. After the bell rang to announce that lunch was over, Bella, Lynn, Kate, and I quickly got up, bussed our table, and ran to the principal's office. We entered the principal's office, and I sat in a chair in front of the desk.

"What is it, girls?" asked Mrs. Smith. (Our principal)

"Mrs. Smith, we have something to show you," said Bella while handing her the phone.

"During lunch, we showed a video that Gina took of us, but we said it was a movie we made. You see, during the break, my friends and I went to this island, and we got powers from a cave," I started.

"And recently, Gina threatened Mary Ann to stay away from Shawn Jones. After the video, Gina walked up to Mary Ann and said this," Bella said, tapping a screen on her phone to start a video she took of Gina.

"Thank you for telling me, girls. I will get Gina's parents on the phone and make sure this never happens again. Now get to class. You don't want to be tardy. Oh, and Mary Ann, if anyone ever picks on you again, please come straight to me, okay?" asked Mrs. Smith.

"Okay," I said in agreement.

"I can't believe that plan worked!" Kate said excitedly.

"Yeah, and guys, thanks for always having my back," I said.

"Hey, it's what best friends do," said Lynn. Then, suddenly, there was a hand on my shoulder.

"Mary Ann!" said the voice. I twirled around to see Gina glaring at me furiously.

"You told the principal on me?" said Gina angrily.

"Yes, I did," I replied calmly.

"Why?" asked Gina.

I took a deep breath and then replied, "Because ever since I started coming to school here, you have been such a jerk to me for no good reason. I put up with you for years, but threatening and spying on me? You have crossed the line Gina, and I'm done putting up with you."

Gina sighed and tilted her head down to look at her feet, and even though I couldn't see the expression on her face, I somehow knew that she felt sad, and I instantly felt terrible for yelling at her. Then, finally, Gina looked up, and I could see her trying to fight back the tears; she walked over to the closest bench in the hall and sat down.

I walked over, sat down next to her, and said softly, "Gina? What's wrong?"

Gina turned around to face me and said, "it's just…my parents always push me so hard to be the best. Be the best at soccer and math, make the best grade in the class, be the prettiest, and be the most popular. It just makes me feel like no matter what I do; I can't please them and let them down. But then I got a lot of friends. I was popular, and I finally felt like I pleased my parents…but you came along, and everybody started hanging out with you, which made me mad. Once again, I couldn't make my parents happy. They always say do whatever it takes to be the best, and that was what I was trying to do…when I started bullying you. I don't know what I thought it would do, but I knew I needed to do something."

"I get it," said Lynn.

"Huh?" said Gina with tears running down her cheeks.

Lynn answered, "I know what it feels like to feel like you can't please your parents. But that doesn't mean you can just take your anger and frustration out on Mary Ann. You know that, right?"

"I do now," said Gina. Then she faced me again and continued, "Mary Ann, I'm so sorry I was so mean to you. I know that all the things I have done to you in the past are tough to forgive, but I hope you can forgive me."

"Oh, Gina, of course, I forgive you. But, trust me, I'm not a person who holds grudges," I replied. Gina chuckled.

"Um, you guys, this forgiveness moment is lovely and stuff, but we have to be in French class in one minute, so maybe you should wrap this up," said Bella checking the watch on her wrist.

"Oh, right, don't want to be late to French now, do we?" I said, standing up and grabbing my backpack.

Gina stood up quickly and said, "Wait, Mary Ann, just a sec. Um, again, I'm sorry for all the things that I did, and I hope that we can be friends?"

"Of course. But maybe we should take the friendship a little slow. I still get nervous around you," I answered. And with that, I threw my backpack onto my shoulder, and Bella and I raced to French class.

Chapter 13

Another Secret

After school, Kate, Bella, Lynn, and I sat in Lynn's bedroom playing Go Fish. (Or my friends were playing while I was deep in thought.)

"Mary Ann, are you okay?" asked Kate. I replied, "Huh? Oh, yeah, I-I'm fine. I was just thinking…didn't it seem weird to you guys how the principal didn't question our powers after we showed her the video?"

There was a minute of silence, but then I was broken by Lynn saying, "Yeah. I guess I never thought about it."

Nobody said a word for a few more minutes until Bella said, "Oh, um, I better get home. I'm helping mom cook dinner tonight. Bye guys!"

"Bye!" my friends and I hollered back as Bella walked out the bedroom door. Shortly after, Kate and I left too; while Kate went back home, I hopped back on my bike and rode to my principal's house. I pushed the doorbell. Ding, Dong!

"Oh, hello, Mary Ann," said Mrs. Smith once she opened the door.

"Hi, Mrs. Smith," I replied, "I was hoping I could ask you a few questions."

"Of course, Mary Ann, come on in," said Mrs. Smith. After I sat on a comfy couch in the den and was served a glass of pink lemonade, I asked, "So, earlier today, when my friends and I told you about our powers…

I mean, I don't want to be rude, but why didn't you seem shocked? I thought you wouldn't believe me, but you did. You acted like this kind of thing happens every day."

Mrs. Smith set down her glass of lemonade and said, "Mary Ann, I didn't question your powers because…well, because I have powers of my own."

It was just a shock to me that I started choking on the lemonade in my mouth, but when I finally caught my breath, I said, "YOU WHAT?"

Mrs. Smith chuckled softly and said, "Yes, Mary Ann, I have powers of my own."

I didn't reply. I just sat there open-mouthed. Then, a few seconds later, Mrs. Smith got a creeped-out expression and said, "Mary Ann, please blink. You're starting to scare me."

I blinked once, maybe twice, but I was so surprised that I couldn't speak! Finally, after what felt like thirty minutes but was probably only a few seconds, I let out a breath I didn't know I was holding, stood up, and said, "I don't think I heard you correctly; you have powers of your own?"

Mrs. Smith patted her hand on the couch seat next to her as if to tell me to sit down. I walked over and sat down next to her. Mrs. Smith turned to face me and put my hands in hers. The way she was sitting made her look like the queen of England or something.

"Mary Ann, I know that you're in shock right now. I mean, this isn't something you hear every day, especially not from your principal, but I need all the thoughts in your head to go away so you can listen to me," said Mrs. Smith.

I took a deep breath, trying to calm myself down then said, "Okay, I'm listening."

"I know it's hard to believe, but you must trust me on this," said Mrs. Smith.

"What powers do you have?" I asked.

"Close your eyes, and think of three things," Mrs. Smith instructed.

I did so, and once I was done, I opened my eyes and said, "Okay, got it." My principal closed her eyes and said, "You were thinking of… Unicorns…Koalas…and…jellybeans."

"That's exactly right!" I cried in amazement. Mrs. Smith chuckled softly and grinned.

"So, should I tell my friends about this? Like about you having powers and stuff?" I asked.

"Well, they have powers too. I think they should know," replied Mrs. Smith.

"Okay, well, I will tell the girls about this then. Anyway, I better get going. I don't want to miss dinner," I said. So, Mrs. Smith walked me to the door, and once I stepped onto the porch, Mrs. Smith called after me, saying, "Mary Ann, make sure that the next time you talk to your friends, tell them that I'm always here to talk if you need to. Oh, and do you need me to drive you home?"

"I will tell the girls, and no, thank you. I have my bike, and my neighborhood isn't far from here." With that, I turned, hopped on my bike, and started riding away, heading toward my house.

When I got home, the first thing I did was go apologize to Mark. I knocked on his bedroom door. Then, assuming he wouldn't reply to the knock, I opened the door.

"Don't you know how to knock?" Mark asked with a sad tone.

I didn't bother to point out that I had knocked. I only said, "I'm sorry." Mark sat up on his bed but didn't say anything, so I continued, "I'm sorry for everything. I shouldn't have yelled at you. Especially in front of all the kids in my school. I'm sorry. The thing is, I told you I could handle it, but you didn't listen. You never listen. You've always been overprotective of me for as long as I can remember." I sat next to Mark and continued, "Mark, I want you to understand that I'm not five anymore. I'm a teenager now. I'm getting more and more responsible every day, and I can stand on my own two feet.

"I know, and I'm sorry too. Ever since I could walk, I've wanted a sibling that I could look out for, and at the time, Brian didn't like me," Mark paused. "But then you came along. I realized I finally had a sibling that I could look out for, and having you brought Brian and me closer together." I leaned closer to my brother and rested my head against his shoulder, and he wrapped his arms around me to hug me. We made up, and I finally made Mark see that I wasn't a little kid anymore.

Chapter 14

Asking Questions

That night after dinner, I went to my room, sat on my bed, and texted my friends to tell them the news.

"NO WAY!" texted Lynn.

"YOU'RE KIDDING!" answered Bella.

"AWESOME!" said Kate. I started to reply but thought, How did my principal get powers? Did she go into the same cave we did? Was she born with these powers? I didn't have an answer to any of my questions, so I texted the girls and asked what they thought.

"IDK, but now that you mention it…maybe we should ask her these questions the next time we talk to her." That was the answer I got from Kate. Lynn and Bella just said, "IDK." A few minutes after Lynn texted, "sorry guys, gtg see you guys tomorrow!" we said our goodbyes to Lynn, then Bella and Kate had to go, so we decided to continue the conversation later.

The next day at school, my friends and I tried our hardest to talk to Mrs. Smith whenever we could. Before school, between classes, before and after lunch, and after school, she was always busy, and we didn't want to interfere with her job just to ask her about her powers. Later at three o'clock, the school bell rang to announce that the school day was over. I packed up my art stuff and rushed out the classroom door because my friends and I had agreed to meet at the door. When I got to the door, I saw Kate, Bella, and Lynn waiting impatiently for me.

"There you are! Where have you been?!" Kate yelled accusingly.

"Well, excuse me, but my classroom isn't across the hall from the door because my classroom is on the second floor on the other side of the building!" I snapped back.

"GIRLS!" screamed Lynn. "We're not here to argue. We're here to talk to Mrs. Smith if we can find her."

"Sorry," Kate whispered to Lynn. Bella sighed loudly, walked up behind Kate, and pushed Kate hard toward me.

"Hug, now!" demanded Bella. Kate and I hugged, and both said we were sorry for yelling. After a minute or so, I asked,

"What if we can't find Mrs. Smith?" Before anybody could answer me, Mrs. Smith walked out in front of us.

"Mrs. Smith!" cried Bella.

"Hello, girls," replied our principal. As our principal walked down the steps, my friends and I followed, asking her the questions.

"Mrs. Smith, we wanted to ask you some questions!" I called.

"About your powers, did you go into the same cave we did?" asked Kate.

"Or were you born with your powers?" asked Lynn.

"How do you handle keeping it secret?" asked Bella.

We were halfway down the stairs when Mrs. Smith stopped and stared around us.

"What are you doing?" I asked. Finally, Mrs. Smith turned to face us and said, "We can't talk here. Walk with me, and we can talk in the park or something." So we started walking, and after about a block or two,

74

Mrs. Smith answered our questions.

But that's a story for next time...

www.ingramcontent.com/pod-product-compliance
Lightning Source LLC
Chambersburg PA
CBHW022051170626
46808CB00003B/1441